Kangaro Surprise

by Maria Velasquez

illustrated by
Richard C. Harrington

Harcourt

Orlando Boston Dallas Chicago San Diego

www.harcourtschool.com

What do you have?

I have a key.

What do you have?

I have a box.

What do you have?

I have a jump rope.